THE LOST TREASURE
OF WALES

JAMES ROOSE-EVANS

THE LOST TREASURE OF WALES

AN ODD & ELSEWHERE STORY:
PICTURES BY BRIAN ROBB

ANDRE DEUTSCH

First published 1977 by
André Deutsch Limited
105 Great Russell Street, London WC1

Printed in Great Britain by
Cox & Wyman Ltd
London, Fakenham and Reading

ISBN 0 233 96784 2

FOR PAM ROYDS, MY EDITOR,
WITH GRATITUDE.

The seven books of Odd and Elsewhere are

THE ADVENTURES OF ODD AND ELSEWHERE
THE SECRET OF THE SEVEN BRIGHT SHINERS
ODD AND THE GREAT BEAR
ELSEWHERE AND THE GATHERING OF THE CLOWNS
THE RETURN OF THE GREAT BEAR
THE SECRET OF TIPPITY-WITCHIT
THE LOST TREASURE OF WALES

*Fenton House is a property
of the National Trust*

'Why, it'll be just like old times!' laughed Odd, clapping his paws in excitement.

Elsewhere was due back that day from his travels. Collander Moll had dusted the house from attic to basement and Odd had polished all the banisters by sliding down them. Now, down in the kitchen, Collander Moll was busy making cakes and tarts while Odd made a special trifle.

Elsewhere, his friend, was King of the Clowns and had been on a trip around the world visiting other clowns. From each country he had sent Odd a postcard. The first card had been numbered *No. 1* and had begun, *'Dear Odd . . .'* The last card, *No. 75*, had arrived that morning and it had said, *'Home next Tuesday for tea. Love, Elsewhere.'* Today was Tuesday.

When all the tarts and cakes were in the oven, Odd collected up the mixing bowls and spoons, first licking them clean, then piling them in the sink.

'I'll do the washing up,' he said.

'Oh, there's a treasure, you are!' beamed Collander Moll, wisps of hair sticking to her damp face like cracks in a wall.

'Am I a treasure?' laughed Odd. 'No one's ever called me that before! If I were a treasure,' he continued, 'surely I'd be made of gold and silver, and my eyes would be made of amber, and my teeth of pearls?'

'There's treasures and treasure,' answered Collander Moll. 'And you are a treasure. Close your eyes!'

Obediently Odd shut his eyes.

'Open your mouth wide!'

Obediently Odd opened his mouth.

'There's treats for being a treasure!' laughed Collander Moll, popping a still warm treacle tart into his mouth.

The kitchen door banged and Hallelujah Jones entered from the garden. Hallelujah was the gardener at Fenton House in Hampstead, and Collander Moll was the housekeeper.

'Where's my tea, girl?' he called. 'And my ginger biscuit!'

'Oh, Dad!' exclaimed Moll. 'I haven't time this afternoon.'

Slowly Hallelujah eased himself into his chair by the fire.

'Oh, my back, my back, boy bach!' he groaned. 'I don't think I can go on with that garden much longer. It's all that stooping. Once I get down I can't get up!'

'Is it your rheumatism?' asked Odd, drying the pots and pans.

'That's it, boy bach! That and me old bones. Getting on, you know. I'm not as young as when you first met me.'

'None of us are!' replied Odd with a grin, hanging up the tea towel behind the door.

'If only I could find something for my rheumatics!' sighed Hallelujah. 'You wouldn't like to rub some of that lotion on my back, would you, girl? The stuff I bought from that gipsy.'

'No, I would not!' replied Collander Moll. 'It stinks the place out!'

Odd looked up from laying the table.

'It says in Elsewhere's big book that I've been reading that gipsies in Hungary train bears to walk up and down people's backs to cure them of rheumatism.'

Hallelujah peered at Odd over his spectacles.

'Is that so, boy bach? You think if you was to walk up and down my back that would do the trick?'

'I could try,' answered Odd.

'I'm not having you on the kitchen floor, Dad, just when I've cleaned it, and Odd walking all over you. There's rubbish I never heard such in my life!' snorted

Collander Moll.

But Hallelujah had pushed the table to one side and was slowly getting down onto the floor.

'I doubt I'll ever get up again!' he puffed. 'But I'm willing to try. Go on, Odd.'

Odd stepped very gently onto Hallelujah's back.

'A bit harder!' grunted Hallelujah. 'Jump about a bit. You know – loosen up the old bones. Don't be afraid.'

As Odd jigged up and down Hallelujah's spine he sang a song,

> *I be a bear*
> *That's busy as a bee:*
> *With a buzz-buzz here,*
> *And a buzz-buzz there,*
> *And a buzz-buzz everywhere!*

On every *buzz* Odd gave a little jump and Hallelujah groaned.

'Oh, Dad!' wailed Collander Moll, 'don't say he's broken your back. Odd, stop it, stop it at once!'

But Odd went on jumping and Hallelujah went on groaning and Moll went on wailing. Suddenly the kitchen door opened and there stood Elsewhere, laden with presents for Odd and Collander Moll and Hallelujah. He put down the presents and clapped his hands.

'Bravo!' he shouted. 'Is this a new act you are rehearsing?'

'Elsewhere!' cried Odd, landing with an extra big thump on Hallelujah's back, and then running to give his friend a hug. He explained what he had been doing.

'But that's big bears, really big bears, that do that,' said Elsewhere.

'You're not thinking of taking Dad to the Zoo, are you?' questioned Collander Moll. 'I mean, he might get mauled to death. Oh, Dad, don't risk it!' she sobbed. 'It's not worth it. What's a few aches and pains now and then to being mauled to death by a bear in the London Zoo. Mind you,' she added, running her duster along the mantelpiece, 'I've always liked Polar bears!'

'Oh, hush, girl!' cried Hallelujah, getting up from the floor. Once Moll got an idea in her head there was no stopping her. 'Nobody's said anything about the Zoo. Have you?' he added, turning to Elsewhere.

'No,' replied Elsewhere. 'It has to be a bear that knows about these things. Each vertebrae has to be clicked into place.'

Hallelujah peered at him.

'You're thinking of the Great Bear, aren't you?' he said.

'Yes,' answered Elsewhere. 'Somehow I think he would know how to do it.'

The Great Bear was Odd's especial friend and he lived in an old chapel in a forest in Wales.

'Why don't you and Odd and Moll come along with me?' suggested Elsewhere to Hallelujah. 'I'm on my way to Tippity House so I could drop you off at the Great Bear's.'

Tippity House was where the King of the Clowns always lived when he was not travelling.

'I feel like a bit of a holiday, then,' replied Hallelujah, looking firmly at Collander Moll. 'I think I'll go and spend a few days with your auntie outside Llandrindod Wells.'

'There's no bears in Llandrindod!' said Moll huffily.

'No, but the Great Bear lives not far away,' replied Odd. 'And I could go and stay with Farmer Thomas and his family. I'll go upstairs and pack a few things!' he announced.

Collander Moll stared after him as he went up the back stairs.

'Oh, there's changed he is!' she cried. 'He used to be such a nice unassuming bear. But now he seems almost grown up. Got a mind of his own. There's determined he is! It's all your doing!' she snapped at Hallelujah. 'It's you encouraged him. He'd never heard of the Great Bear until you told him.'

Hallelujah pretended not to hear.

'By the way, Moll,' he said, winking at Elsewhere, 'don't forget to pack my spare set of false teeth, in case I decide to go to chapel on Sunday!'

Outside Fenton House stood the King's caravan, with a horse standing between the shafts, munching from a bag of oats. The caravan was carved and painted with birds, fishes, fruit and flowers. On the four corners of the roof were lion's heads which served as gargoyles. When it rained the water slid down the roof and out through the mouths of the lions.

Collander Moll staggered backwards and forwards from the house to the caravan, carrying loads of food; fresh baked bread, butter, cheese, bottles of home made chutney, tins full of cakes and biscuits, thermos flasks of soup and tea and coffee and hot milk.

Hallelujah stood staring at her as she bustled, warm and perspiring, up and down the basement steps. 'There's mad you are, girl! Anyone would think we were setting off for the North Pole! We're only going to Wales for the weekend!'

Moll's mad eyes flashed. 'You never know when you may be held up!' she answered. 'There's traffic wardens, and fogs, and hi-jackers, and hitch-hikers, and summer storms, and spring cleanings. Not to mention highway-

men!'

Finally everything was loaded on board. Collander Moll locked up the house and slipped the big key into her pocket. The others were already seated at the front of the caravan, waiting for her.

'Ups-a-daisy!' they cried, as all three heaved her on board. It was already dusk, and Elsewhere had lit the lamps. He always travelled at night when there was less traffic on the roads and he could go at a brisker trot.

As they journeyed, he told them stories of his travels. Wherever he had gone he had called together a special Gathering of Clowns. In the past, Gatherings had been

14

held only on rare occasions, such as the crowning of a
new king, and then the clowns had come from all over
the world to gather at Tippity House.

'But I decided to change things,' explained Elsewhere.
'I thought, when I became King, that it would be fun
to have lots of smaller Gatherings so that when there
had to be a really big Gathering everyone would already
know each other.'

He told them how he had found clowns in the heart
of Africa, as well as in tiny villages in Persia. In Greece
he had gone sailing in a boat from island to island, in
search of one little known group of clowns who were

said to be descended from 'The Frogs', those comic actors who had worked in Athens in the fourth century B.C.

'And then at last we saw them. They were travelling in a small cart drawn by a horse. Fixed to the cart were parasols to protect them from the sun. Even the horse had a straw hat with holes pierced in it so that its ears could stick through. They live on one of the tiniest islands in the Peloponnese and they have promised to come to the next large Gathering.'

One by one the stars came out and soon they were out in the country, with the smell of spring everywhere, and the sound of birds chirping in their sleep.

'Look!' cried Odd suddenly. The road wound through a wood and ahead of them, through the trees, they could see lights moving.

'Could they be flying glow-worms?' asked Elsewhere.

'Listen!' said Odd.

Drifting through the trees, came a sound like that of tiny bagpipes playing a lament, soft and far away. This was followed by a succession of quivering notes like the plucking of bow strings. Lastly there was a cascade of notes as though someone were playing a harp. The different sounds began to weave in and out, forming a pattern.

Hallelujah cocked his head at Collander Moll and said,

'Know what it reminds me of, Moll?'

Collander Moll nodded, her eyes shining with excitement.

'One of our *nosen llawen*, Dad!'

'What's – whatever that is?' asked Elsewhere.

'It means "a merry evening" in Welsh. Everyone gets

together to make music, sing and recite. Dad and me used to be known all over the valleys. Dad would play the harp – oh, beautiful it was before his fingers grew too stiff – and I would sing. I was a lovely contralto, wasn't I, Dad?'

'Aye, lovely she was!' replied Hallelujah, nodding in agreement. He blew out a puff of smoke from his pipe and added, 'That's a harp, for sure, that someone is playing now. A Welsh harp, too.'

The next moment they rounded a corner and there, in a clearing, set back from the road, was a small group of clowns, all dressed in white, like miniature druids, with white veils draped over their heads. One of them was playing a small harp, one a pipe made from a cow's horn, and the third drew a bow across strings fixed to a wooden box. Hung in the holly trees round about were paraffin lanterns. The flames were reflected in the shiny, wet-looking dark holly leaves. Moths darted in and out causing shadows.

'I forgot to tell you,' laughed Elsewhere on seeing the small group, 'that I've called a Gathering of the Welsh clowns and I promised to give any who wanted a lift on

my way to Tippity House.'

When the Welsh clowns saw the King's caravan approaching, their leader, who had a face like a carved turnip, cried out, '*Joseph*!'

At once Elsewhere, acknowledging the clowns' password, replied, '*Grimaldi*!'

The first clown stepped forward and said, 'I am Hywel-ap-Hywel. These are Llewellyn, Dafydd, Owen, and Huw, and this is Morgan.'

One after the other they all shook hands, chattering away in Welsh to Hallelujah and Collander Moll. Then they took down their lanterns and hung them from the sides of the caravan.

'Tea everyone?' cooed Collander Moll, lighting the primus stove in the back of the caravan. Moll always liked company.

'Oh, there's lovely then!' grinned Hywel-ap-Hywel.

'We were practising for the Gathering,' said Owen.

'Regular Eisteddfod we were having!' laughed Dafydd.

And so, all through the night, from Abergavenny to Crickhowell, from Talgarth to Builth Wells, they stopped to pick up other groups of clowns, until the caravan was crowded inside and out with clowns chattering away in Welsh. They sang all the famous Welsh songs including Collander Moll's favourite hymn, *Cwm Rhondda*. The sun was just rising as they approached Llandrindod Wells singing – *Sospan Fach*!

They dropped off Collander Moll at her auntie's, Miss Myfanwy Price, and then drove on up into Radnor Forest until they came to a farm tucked beneath the crest of a hill, sheltered by trees. From one chimney, smoke softly filtered, and they knew by this that Farmer Thomas was up.

He was one of Odd's especial friends and had helped him find the Great Bear when he had first come to Wales. Farmer Thomas, Mrs Thomas, and all their children, some still in their pyjamas and rubbing the sleep from their eyes, crowded to the door to stare up at the colourful caravan full of clowns. Farmer Thomas grinned at Elsewhere and Odd.

'There's welcome back you are!' he said to Elsewhere. 'Come you on in!'

They all tumbled out of the caravan and Mrs Thomas made breakfast for everyone. They sat down at the large kitchen table, bringing in extra benches from the front parlour, and helped themselves to rashers of bacon from a big blue and white dish in the centre of the table. Then they dipped slices of bread into the hot bacon fat. It was a fine Spring morning and doors and windows were left open. Hens clucked their way indoors, while the dogs wagged their tails and waited, bright-eyed, for titbits.

Odd introduced Hallelujah and explained about his rheumatism and how they hoped the Great Bear might be able to cure it.

'After breakfast,' Farmer Thomas offered, 'I'll drive you and Hallelujah to the Great Bear's, while Elsewhere goes on to Tippity House with the others.'

Elsewhere looked up from the head of the table where he had been entertaining the children with conjuring tricks.

'I'll call for you at the Great Bear's tomorrow morning,' he said to Odd.

The Great Bear had moved down from his hut on Bear Mountain and gone to live in Merlin's Chapel in Brockland Forest, at the foot of the mountain. Here he gardened, kept bees, bottled his own fruit, made jams, and brewed his own wine.

That morning he was making himself a pancake. He was very partial to pancakes smothered with honey from his own hives. He was pouring the batter carefully into a heated pan when there was a sharp knock at his front door and a voice shouted, 'Your bees are swarming!'

'Oh, Lord! Not another lot!' exclaimed the Great Bear. He hurried to the front door, holding the pan in one paw. On the doorstep stood Farmer Thomas, Odd, and an old man in a faded policeman's uniform.

'Why, it's Ursus Minor, the Little Bear!' he cried, reaching out to shake Odd by the paw, and forgetting that he was still holding the frying pan. The pancake flew through the air and landed on top of Hallelujah's helmet.

'Keep the pancake on!' shouted the Great Bear. 'It'll

do as a bee veil. We've no time to lose.'

Quickly he pulled down some net curtains from a window and handed them to Odd and Farmer Thomas.

'Here, you two. Wrap these around your heads. And keep your hands, or paws, in your pockets. The bees don't sting me because they're used to me, but strangers can be another matter.'

He hurried up the steep garden, past the vegetable patch and the blackcurrant and gooseberry bushes, to the small orchard at the top. A large lump, like boiling treacle, seemed to be oozing out of the branch of an apple tree. Odd gazed up at the shining brown and buzzing mass of bees.

'The Queen is in the middle of that,' said the Great Bear, laying a white cloth on the grass underneath the swarm. 'If she were to fly off, the others would follow. They could fly a mile or two away and then I should probably lose them.'

He held a straw skep under the swarm and gave the branch a vigorous shake. The sticky shape fell in buzzing lumps into the open basket. Then he placed the skep mouth downwards on the white cloth, propping it up on one side so that the bees could come and go.

'We'll leave them there in the shade,' he said, 'until it's dusk. Then I'll move them into a new hive.'

He led the way back to the house, pausing to have a look to see how his rhubarb was growing under two large enamel bowls.

'Now, after all that excitement,' he said, 'I suggest we have a glass of home-made wine.'

A muffled voice murmured, 'Might I take this off now?'

The Great Bear turned to find Hallelujah struggling

with the pancake which hung round his face.

'It must be cooked by now,' he said. 'We'll eat some with our wine.'

They sat round the kitchen table and broke off pieces of honeycomb to eat with the pancake while they sampled different wines.

'Take your choice,' said the Great Bear. 'There's crab-apple, clover, strawberry, elderberry (very good for colds!), nettle, grass, dandelion – there's even potato wine. You can make wine out of almost anything. Even tea leaves! And now,' he added, turning to Odd, 'what brings you here?'

'It's Hallelujah's back,' said Odd, and he explained to the Great Bear about Hallelujah's rheumatism.

'Oh, there's painful it is!' said Hallelujah cheerfully, pouring himself some more dandelion wine. 'There's this pain, you see, it gets me in the back when I'm not

looking for it. It's a regular zigzag, like lightning. It starts here,' he explained, like a guide on a tour, 'right up on my left shoulder and from there it travels across the shoulder-blades, runs down my back, past the kidneys, slips slyly round the side, and sinks suddenly to the bottom. Oh, it quite takes my breath away sometimes!'

'And so,' continued Odd, 'We thought perhaps you might know how to walk up and down his back like the bears do in Elsewhere's book at home.'

'I don't know about that,' answered the Great Bear. 'I might break every bone in his body! But I do have another cure (and the very best there is) for rheumatism.'

'What is that?' asked Odd.

'Bees!' replied the Great Bear.

'Where?' cried Hallelujah in alarm, slamming his helmet back onto his head.

'A few bee stings in the affected areas,' explained the Great Bear, 'and you'll be fit as a fiddle.'

He rose and went outside.

'I'm not being stung by bees, that's for certain!' cried Hallelujah, pouring himself another glass of wine.

'You want to watch that stuff you're drinking!' grinned Farmer Thomas.

The Great Bear returned with a jam jar in the bottom of which crawled six large bees.

'You'll have to get undressed,' he said to Hallelujah.

Hallelujah went red in the face and burst into Welsh. He had never been known to take off his clothes. Farmer Thomas winked at Odd and whispered, 'I think we'd better go outside!'

Standing among the Great Bear's apple trees, they could hear above the steady hum of bees, the protests of Hallelujah as the Great Bear made him get undressed. There was a pause and then they heard a loud roar. Six times Hallelujah roared as the Great Bear applied the bees. Then there was a long silence.

The Great Bear came outside.

'I've given him something to make him sleep,' he smiled. 'When he wakes up he will have forgotten he ever had any trouble with his back.'

While the Great Bear was speaking, Odd had been staring, puzzled, up at Bear Mountain which he could glimpse above the tops of the trees of the Forest. The

Great Bear glanced at him. 'So you've noticed it as well?'

'It's the mist at the top, isn't it?' answered Odd. 'It's almost as though it were thinning out.'

They stood staring up at the mountain. Mist was swirling about the summit like clouds of steam from a saucepan of boiling water, and every now and then they could glimpse a dark shape.

'It's almost as though the mist were going to lift at any minute,' observed Farmer Thomas. 'Now that's strange. The mountain's always been shrouded in mist as long as anyone can remember. That's why it's always had a bad name, as though it were trying to hide something. That's why it's been known as Black Mountain, although we know that its real name is Bear Mountain.'

'Do you think it has anything to do with Malevil?' asked Odd.

Malevil was their most feared enemy. He had long sought the Lost Treasure of Wales which was supposed to lie hidden inside the mountain. The Great Bear had always said that one day Malevil would return to make another attempt to find the treasure.

The Great Bear shook his head. 'There's been no sign of Malevil,' he said. 'Although Farmer Thomas tells me there have been rumours of vehicles heard moving about on the mountain at night, without lights.'

'But no one is certain,' added Farmer Thomas. 'For one thing, as you know, no one round here will go anywhere near the mountain at night.'

The Great Bear sighed. 'If only I could see what is behind that mist! It's reminding me of something but I can't think what.'

26

'How would we know if Malevil were back?' asked Odd of Farmer Thomas as they drove in to town to do some shopping while Hallelujah was sleeping.

'If Malevil does return,' replied Farmer Thomas, 'I reckon he won't make such a show as he did last time with guards and barricades and searchlights. Regular show off that was. No, this time I'd say he'll be a bit more subtle. We might not even know he was in our midst – leastways not until it was too late.'

'You mean,' said Odd, 'that Malevil might be in disguise?'

'Yes,' answered Farmer Thomas. 'Malevil could disguise himself and we'd never recognise him. He might be here right now and us not know it.'

Odd peered out at the little groups of farmers and their wives in the main street of the crowded market town. Their voices rose and fell softly as they stood gossiping in Welsh. He wondered if one of them might be Malevil.

'Of course,' he said thoughtfully, 'there is one thing that Malevil can't disguise and that is his missing eye.'

'You are right there,' replied Farmer Thomas. 'However he disguised himself, he'd have to use an eye-patch, or spectacles of some kind. In that sense he is a marked man, so that should make it easier for us to detect him.'

In the centre of the town was a small covered medieval market place and here Odd found his friend, Mr Goodman, serving behind a stall across the top of which was a large sign which read

GRANARY PRODUCE

On the stall were baskets of brown Granary eggs; Granary butter splashed with water and resting on beds of green leaves; jars of *Odd's Own Honey*, named especially after him; wholemeal bread, Radnor cheeses, and tubs full of herbs for use in salads. Mr Goodman was wearing a butcher's striped blue and white apron. His sleeves were rolled up and he had a straw hat tilted on the back of his head.

'All home grown, Granary fresh!' he was shouting

out as he served the customers, ringing up the change on an old fashioned silver-plated cash register that had been converted to decimal coinage. He seemed to have a word for everyone, even for small children who only wanted half an ounce of home made Granary fudge.

Mr Goodman had once been Keeper of the British Railways Lost Property Office in London, but when it had been burgled he had decided to give up lost property and take up butterfly breeding. With his assistant, Arbuthnot, he had moved to Wales, not far from Farmer Thomas, to live at the Granary where he had since started a farm.

'Hullo, Odd!' he called out. 'You've arrived just in time. I've got some young customers here asking for your honey.'

Soon Odd was busy selling small pots of *Odd's Own Honey* to a long queue of children. Farmer Thomas left him to go off to the cattle market.

'Where's Arbuthnot?' asked Odd.

'He stayed behind at the Granary,' replied Mr Goodman, weighing a large slab of cheese for a farmer who

29

had shiny red cheeks and looked uncomfortable in a starched white collar. 'A large batch of orders came in this morning for butterfly eggs and caterpillars. Our butterfly business is really booming. Haven't you noticed that there are many more butterflies about?'

Mr Goodman paused and looked around the market hall where the other owners of stalls were quietly munching sandwiches and drinking cups of tea.

'That's funny!' he remarked. 'I wonder where everyone has vanished to all of a sudden?'

Farmer Thomas returned.

'Where is everyone?' asked Mr Goodman.

Farmer Thomas laughed.

'They've all gone to look at the latest attraction – Dr Bounder and his Instant Brew! He's a quack medicine man. He claims his medicine is a cure for everything from warts to rheumatism.'

'Perhaps he might have cured Hallelujah,' suggested Odd.

Farmer Thomas chuckled. 'It's only coloured water, you know! There used to be chaps like him about when I was your age. They'd travel round the country, visiting markets and fairs, but they'd take care not to appear too often in the same place. The idea is to make a quick sale and then clear out. Why don't you run along, Odd, and have a look for yourself? It's as good as an entertainment!'

When Odd came out of the market place he found the street crowded, but long before he could see anything he could hear Dr Bounder.

'Ladies and gentlemen! Boys and girls!' he was saying. 'I am here to tell you that crowned heads of Europe have been cured by my medicine! Lords and ladies up and down the land, schoolboys with their homework problems, wives with errant husbands, husbands with errant wives, all have been helped.

'Whatever your problem, be it falling hair or failing sight, pubescent spots or poor circulation; for all ailments of the bladder, bowel or brain, I guarantee you that a spoonful of Dr Bounder's Instant Brew will solve your problems overnight!'

Odd worked his way through to the front of the crowd where he found a stall decorated with photographs of the crowned heads of Europe, as well as framed testimonials from individuals stating that Dr Bounder's Instant Brew had cured their rheumatism, neuralgia, insomnia or whatever. They were signed: I. B. Betta of Plymouth; Eva Sigh of Relief; Ida Cold of Taunton and U. R. Topps of Chester. At the back of the stall were hundreds of medicine bottles filled with a bright pink liquid.

'Only twenty five new pence a bottle!' cried Dr Bounder. 'Hurry! Hurry! Hurry! Absolutely unrepeatable offer!'

He was standing to one side of the stall, handing out bottles of the medicine as the crowd surged round him.

He was wearing a black frock coat, green with age, with a waistcoat made from a Union Jack flag, and around his top hat was a band with the words – Dr Bounder's Instant Brew.

But what caught Odd's attention and made him gasp, was the fact that his eyes were hidden behind dark pink spectacles. Quickly, so that he should not be seen, he shrank back between a large lady and an elderly clergyman. If this were Malevil in disguise, and he was almost certain it must be, he must slip away before he was noticed.

Just as he was about to turn, however, a hand gripped his shoulder and a quiet voice murmured, 'So, my young friend, we meet again!'

Odd looked up, startled, at the elderly clergyman who was bending over him. Beneath his straw hat he wore dark glasses and his face was fringed with white whiskers.

There was a sudden surge from the crowd behind and Odd and the clergyman were parted. At the same moment Dr Bounder was thrown off balance and his pink glasses slipped. It was then Odd saw that both his eyes were normal.

Looking back, he could see the elderly clergyman fighting his way through the crowd towards him. Swiftly Odd ducked, pushing his way between the legs and feet of the crowd, glad for once that he was small. Not knowing who was treading on their feet, the crowd began to argue and fight with those next to them. Angry women hit red-faced farmers over the head with their umbrellas; men fought with each other, until there was pandemonium in the market street.

Odd ran as fast as he could back to the market place.

'What is it, Odd?' asked Mr Goodman. 'You look as if you had seen a ghost!'

'You've not been drinking Dr Bounder's Instant Brew, have you?' joked Farmer Thomas. 'Some do say as how he puts turpentine in it.'

Odd looked up at his two friends. He was shaking all over. It was not until then that he realised how frightened he had been.

'It's Malevil!' he cried. 'He has returned. I've just seen him. He's disguised as an elderly clergyman.'

In his first attempt to find the Lost Treasure of Wales, Malevil had been badly defeated by the Great Bear. Now he had returned, but with greater guile, to make a second attempt. Under cover of darkness he had silently moved his men into the mountain, determined that this time the Great Bear should have no suspicion of his presence on, or in, the mountain.

When Malevil had discovered that the interior of the mountain was a maze of tunnels, he had sent for his chief officer, Ratzwill, a mournful little man who had a nervous habit of plucking at the hairs on the insides of his nostrils.

'Our first task,' said Malevil, 'is to make a map of the interior of this mountain, every tunnel, passage, cave and recess. Once we have such a map I am convinced we shall have the key to the whereabouts of the Treasure.'

Days, weeks, went by, however, and each time Malevil asked Ratzwill what progress was being made, the latter merely tugged more nervously at the hairs inside his nose, replying dryly that there were a lot of tunnels in the mountain. The mountain, he said, was like the inside of a bee hive.

Now Malevil sat, drumming his fingers on a trestle table in the cave which served as his temporary head-quarters. He was angry that he had given himself away by acting on an impulse and speaking to Odd. He did not doubt that Odd had recognised him and that, within a short space of time, the Great Bear would be alerted that he, Malevil, had returned to the neigh-bourhood, even if they did not suspect that he had set up camp inside the mountain. Although the enemy were so few and Malevil's forces far outweighed theirs, yet Malevil knew, from his previous experience, that the Great Bear had access to ancient sources of power that he had learned from his master, Merlin.

Abruptly he stopped drumming the table. He pressed a button on the intercom system that had been installed inside the mountain by his engineers.

'Send Commander Ratzwill to me!' he ordered.

He got up and stood in front of a large ordnance sur-

vey map of the whole area including Brockland Forest.
He turned round as Ratzwill entered.

'I want a progress report,' said Malevil. 'And what's
more, you'd better have some progress to report this
time!'

Ratzwill stood silent, plucking at the hairs in his
nose.

'Stop picking your nose!' snapped Malevil.

'I'm not, sir!' answered Ratzwill.

'Yes, you are!' replied Malevil.

'Beg pardon, sir, but I'm not.'

'If you are not picking your nose, Ratzwill, what *are*
you doing?'

'Twirling, sir,' answered Ratzwill.

'Twirling?' echoed Malevil.

'Yes, sir, twirling. I'm twirling the hairs inside my
nostrils. I find it comforting.'

'Well, don't!' answered Malevil. 'It does not comfort
me. Now, I want a progress report.'

'I'm afraid we haven't made much progress, sir.'

'Why not?'

'It's the men, sir. They're saying the mountain is
haunted.'

'Superstitious and insubordinate nonsense!' shouted
Malevil who always got angry when he was opposed.

'If I may venture an opinion, sir?'

Malevil sighed petulantly and sat down.

'Well, go on!' he answered, waving a hand at Ratzwill
to continue.

'Many of the passages inside the mountain appear to
go round in circles, or to peter out at the edge of a
precipice. It's almost as though they had been designed
to lead nowhere. I am convinced that Merlin planned

36

all this very carefully, anticipating that one day someone would attempt to find the treasure. If I am right,
then the Great Bear must have the key to the maze, for
he was Merlin's assistant. And if he has the key then
he has the whereabouts of the treasure.'

Malevil stared at Ratzwill, a slow smile spreading
across his thin face like a scar. It was a smile of sarcasm.

'Precisely!' he answered. 'And Ursus Major, the Great
Bear, has forgotten the key!'

'So he *said*, sir!' replied Ratzwill.

Malevil looked up at his companion, his expression
changing.

'After all,' continued Ratzwill, 'when he escaped from
us last time, it must have been *through* the mountain
since he managed to avoid the sentries and the barricades on the outside; which would mean that he does
know his way about the inside of the mountain; in
which case he must remember where the Treasure is
hidden!'

'In other words,' interrupted Malevil, 'what you are
saying is that the Great Bear has been leading us a
dance in a maze!'

37

'Mind you,' went on Ratzwill, as if he had not heard the interruption, 'it still does not explain one thing.'

'What's that?' asked Malevil.

'If the Great Bear does remember where the Treasure is hidden, why did he not reveal the secret to Ursus Minor, the Little Bear, when he was woken by him, as the legend states he should have done?'

Malevil grunted. He paced up and down and around the cave.

'Of course the legend doesn't say *when* the Treasure is to be found,' ruminated Malevil. 'It only says that a member of the tribe of *Ursus*, or bear, shall waken the Great Bear who will reveal to him the whereabouts of the Lost Treasure of Wales. It could be that the time has not yet come for the Great Bear to reveal its whereabouts and that only when that time comes will he remember.'

Malevil paused and stood staring at Ratzwill. 'But where does the legend come from?' he asked. 'It's not in any of the Arthurian records that I know of. It seems to be something that has been handed down entirely by word of mouth and for all we know may be hearsay unless . . .'

'Yes?' prompted Ratzwill.

'Unless,' replied Malevil, 'it is in *The Book of Merlin.*'

'The Book of Merlin?'

'Yes, the book in which Merlin wrote down all his Prophecies. If the legend is true than it will be there. Why did I not think of this before? I wager my one remaining eye that the Great Bear has a copy. You must go at once to Merlin's Hermitage in the Forest, where the Great Bear now lives, and find that book. Any moment now he will learn from Ursus Minor that I am in the neighbourhood and then he will be on the alert. It will not be so easy, once that happens, to get past his guard. Hurry!'

The Great Bear was looking for a recipe the ingredients of which he had forgotten. While Hallelujah slept, he browsed among his books, enjoying specially those he had inherited from Merlin. Although he had purposely destroyed Merlin's best book of spells lest it should fall into the wrong hands, he had kept the simple remedies and charms, many of which had been written on scraps of paper and pushed inside the covers of books.

From shelf after shelf he pulled out books until they lay in heaps all over the floor. As he turned the pages, dust flew up and settled on his spectacles so that he had to keep stopping to wipe them clean. Sometimes he became so absorbed in a book that he sat in the middle of the floor and quite forgot what it was he was looking for.

He sighed. He had emptied all the shelves and gone through every book and still he had not found the recipe. It was for a special wine made with honey that he wanted to brew for Odd. He got up and ambled over to a pile of old chests and boxes in a far corner of the room. He could not remember what was inside them. With difficulty he opened an ancient and rusty trunk and rummaged about inside it. There were bones, bits of old rock and fossils, a human skull, some Tarot cards, phials that appeared to be empty, and then, at the bottom, he found something large and heavy wrapped in leather.

He lifted it out and carried it to the table. He could not think what it might be. Slowly he unwrapped the leather skin and there before him lay a book the existence of which he had long forgotten, its pages fragile with age and worm-eaten but, none the less, *The Book of Merlin*. It was centuries since he had last looked at it, and now he went back in memory over all that had happened since Merlin had first rescued him from Malevil and taken him to be his assistant at the Court of King Arthur.

Gently he opened the book. Its pages were thin as tissue paper and the ink had faded. He had to use a magnifying glass in order to read the delicate writing. Each of the Prophecies was in a special code the key to which was known only to Merlin and the Great Bear.

Now, once again, he read of Merlin's early days, and

how he had come to set up the Round Table at Carduel in Wales. Slowly he turned the pages. Prophecy after prophecy relating to the future history of the Round Table was there; each of which had been fulfilled, including the Peregrinations of Perceval of Wales, the Coming of Galahad, and the End of the Round Table.

The Great Bear paused, his heart beating swiftly. Then he read clearly the last prophecy of all, concerning the Lost Treasure of Wales. Line by line he decoded it –

When the mists begin to thin,
Then shall you soon espy . . .'

He stared with excitement at the page, holding the magnifying glass closer to the words, trying to decipher the next line. The room darkened as though the sky had clouded over, and he got up to light a lamp. It was then that he noticed someone peering in through one of the small arched windows of the chapel. He wondered who it could be. Few people ever penetrated so far into the Forest and visitors were a rarity.

Outside stood two men. A small van was parked by the gate.

'Any old furniture or books you want to sell?' asked one of the men who stood nervously plucking at the hairs inside his left nostril. 'We're antique dealers and antiquarians.'

He drew the Great Bear to one side, while the other man went round to the back of the building.

'We pay a good price,' said the first man. 'And in cash, too. Means you don't have to declare it on your income tax forms.'

'I don't pay income tax,' answered the Great Bear, puzzled. 'Indeed, I'm not sure what kind of tax that is.'

'Ho, lucky you!' joked the man, nudging him with his elbow and winking. He took out a packet of cigarettes and offered one to the Great Bear who shook his head to say no.

'We go around the farms and cottages mainly,' explained the man, puffing out clouds of smoke that made the Great Bear cough. 'You'd be surprised how many old books we find lying around in attics and cellars, going mildewy with the damp. We export them to America. Big business there. Wealthy Americans, who want to build up a library overnight, write to us and order three or four thousand books. They don't read them – so long as they look old, they're put on their shelves for show.'

'There's nothing I want to sell,' replied the Great Bear, wondering what had happened to the other man.

'It was just that peering through your window,' continued the first man, puffing away, 'to see if anyone was at home, you understand – wouldn't want you to think we were being nosy – I noticed you seemed to have a lot of old books about the place and so we thought, well, maybe you'd like to get rid of a few.'

'Sorry, but I read my books,' replied the Great Bear. 'They are like old friends to me. I should be very grieved to lose any of them, let alone sell them.'

Just then the other man came up, fastening his flies, as though he had been having a pee. He was carrying a large rucksack on his back. The first man looked at his companion and said to the Great Bear,

'Sorry to have troubled you. We'll be getting on our way, then. So long!'

They climbed into their van and drove off along the forest track. Something about their manner troubled the Great Bear but he could not think what it was. He shook his head and turned to look up at the sky. It was already dusk and time to get the swarm of bees into their new hive.

There was a soft hoot and a barn owl flew down
towards him.

'Ah, there you are, Taliesin!' smiled the Great Bear,
greeting the bird, once Merlin's own messenger, and
now his constant companion.

Taliesin flew up to the ivy on the tower of the hermitage and watched the Great Bear going about his task
of gathering the bees.

First he placed a small plank with a white handker-
chief draped over it at the entrance to the new hive,
tilting it down to the ground so that it formed a run-
way. Next he lifted the skep and gently lowered it in
front of the hive, removing the cloth that covered it. In
no time at all the Queen Bee emerged and led all the
other bees up the gang-plank into their new home. Soon
the inside of the hive was humming like an engine.

As the Great Bear straightened up, he saw that he
was no longer alone. Gravely watching him were Odd,
Farmer Thomas, and Mr Goodman. Something about
their silence made him say, 'It's Malevil, isn't it?'

Odd nodded, and told him about his meeting with Malevil. No sooner had he finished than the Great Bear growled deeply and charged downhill towards the house. Lighting a lamp, he pushed his way through the mounds of books until he was standing by – the empty table. He lifted his paw and slammed it down with such a crash, and swore such a mighty oath in Latin, that Hallelujah started up from his sleep, crying out, 'There's such a dream I had! I dreamed as how there was a whole hive of bees inside my helmet!'

He stopped, seeing the troubled, anxious, look on the faces of the others.

'I've been foiled, I've been trapped!' roared the Great Bear. 'I've been an idiot, a clumsy bear. I can see it all now. While the first man was occupying my attention, his accomplice was in here looking for it.'

'What?' asked Odd. 'What was he looking for?'

'*The Book of Merlin!*' answered the Great Bear. 'Only one other person can have known of its existence and that is Malevil!'

'*The Book of Merlin* – what is that?' asked Odd.

'It is the book that contains all the Prophecies of Merlin,' answered the Great Bear.

'But why should Malevil want that?'

'Because it contains the key to the whereabouts of the Treasure, that's why.'

Odd stared at the Great Bear in puzzlement.

'But in that case why didn't you think of it before?'

'Oh, dear, dear me!' sighed the Great Bear. 'I'm ashamed to admit it but I had forgotten all about it! I came across the book by accident this afternoon. I was looking for a special recipe with which to make some honey wine for you, and I found the book at the bottom of that old trunk.'

'I wonder what made Malevil think of it at almost the same time?' said Farmer Thomas thoughtfully.

'Telepathy!' grunted Mr Goodman by way of answer.

'Tele- what?' asked Odd.

'Telepathy. Mind reading. It's a kind of mental radar with which some people are equipped. It sounds to me very probable that so strong was the Great Bear's

47

reaction on finding the book that Malevil picked up the vibrations.'

'Do you mean that Malevil now knows where the Treasure is?' interrupted Odd with a worried expression.

They were sitting round the table in the lamplight.

'No,' answered the Great Bear. 'Fortunately the Prophecies are in a code to which only I have the key . . .'

'But,' interrupted Mr Goodman, 'that places you in great danger!'

'It will not be the first time,' laughed the Great Bear. 'But now that I am alerted to Malevil I can prevent him getting inside my thoughts. More than that, however, I discovered something of vital importance just before I was interrupted by the two men.'

'What was that?' asked Farmer Thomas.

'The reason why the Treasure has not yet been found.'

'What is it?' asked Odd.

'It's really very simple,' answered the Great Bear. 'Until now it has not been the right time for it to be discovered! You see, although the legend always said that the whereabouts of the Treasure would be revealed to the one who woke me from my long sleep, it did not say *when*. I think Malevil may have sensed this and that would explain why he has returned at this time. And once he has succeeded in deciphering the book he will know that the time when the secret of the Treasure will be revealed is now very close at hand.'

The Great Bear chuckled. 'Mind you,' he added, 'I think he's in for a big disappointment! He may find the truth of the proverb – all that glitters is not gold!'

'But what actually did the prophecy say?' grumbled Mr Goodman, anxious lest the Great Bear should now forget what he had set out to tell them.

The Great Bear peered at Mr Goodman over the top of his spectacles, then he declaimed in his deep voice,

> *When the mists begin to thin,*
> *Then shall you soon espy*
> *Merlin's Castle in the sky!*

He paused.

'Is that all?' said Mr Goodman, disappointed.

'It's enough!' rumbled the Great Bear.

'What does it mean?' asked Odd. 'About seeing Merlin's Castle in the sky?'

'Follow me!' answered the Great Bear.

He led them into the tower at the end of the chapel, and up a ladder into a loft where hens were muttering on their roosts, and out through a trapdoor onto the battlements.

High overhead, above the Forest which rustled in the chill night air, the moon, almost at full, sailed among clouds. To one side of it lay the constellations of the Great Bear and the Little Bear. Ahead of them, brilliant in the moonlight, rose Bear Mountain, the mist about its summit stirring like silver veils of incense.

'There!' said the Great Bear softly in the silence of the night. 'There, behind that mist, which until now has always shrouded the summit, and which these past few days has begun to thin, is Merlin's Castle!'

He paused dramatically, and Taliesin, hearing the name of Merlin, feathered softly downwards towards the Great Bear, alighting on his wrist.

'And that,' continued the Great Bear, 'is where the Lost Treasure of Wales is hidden! Until now it has always been hidden by the mist – as was intended by Merlin – which is also why I could not remember where the Treasure was hidden. A case of "out of sight, out of mind"!' he chuckled.

While the Great Bear was speaking, Farmer Thomas had been scanning the mountain with a pair of binoculars.

'I do find it strange,' he remarked, 'knowing as we now do that Malevil has returned, that there's no sign of anything happening on the mountain. Not like last time, remember! Yet if he's not on the mountain, where is he?'

'I wonder!' murmured Odd thoughtfully.

'What?' asked the others.

'He could be *inside* the mountain,' replied Odd.

'You could well be right, Odd!' said the Great Bear.

'And for all we know,' added Farmer Thomas, 'he might be excavating away inside, like an old mole, and we none the wiser. By now he might even be excavating upwards into the summit, and discover the existence of the Castle almost by accident!'

For a moment they stood awed by the thought. Then the Great Bear sighed and said, 'We must go in now and make plans. We have no time to lose.'

Inside the chapel they sat around the kitchen table. Taliesin perched on top of the dresser, his eyes narrowed to slits. Hallelujah lit his pipe and sent puffs of smoke sailing across the table.

'Our first task,' announced the Great Bear, 'is to find out exactly what Malevil is up to. I think Odd is probably right in supposing he may already be inside the mountain. In which case . . .'

He broke off. The room was suddenly full of smoke. Odd looked up, thinking it must be Hallelujah's pipe. The Great Bear rose, thinking it must be the chimney smoking. Thick clouds of white smoke were pouring down the chimney, filling the room like a fog. They stumbled about, coughing and choking.

'Open the door, someone!' shouted Farmer Thomas. 'Open a window!'

'I can't!' answered Mr Goodman. 'They've been barred from the outside.'

51

To Odd it seemed as though the room was full of shapes emerging like shadows from the corners. He could just see that they wore masks around their mouths and noses. The next minute his paws were grabbed from behind and tied with cord, a sack was thrown over his head, and he was hurried outside and into the back of a van. He knew he was not alone because he could hear the others struggling. Finally the door of the van was slammed, the engine started, and they were driven off along the bumpy tracks of the Forest.

The journey seemed endless. The van twisted and changed direction so many times, with sudden changes of gear, and, each time this happened, the friends were rolled about in the back of the van until they were bruised all over. Finally the van stopped, the doors were opened, and they were tumbled out. The sacks were

pulled off their heads and they stood blinking in the glare from a row of arc lamps. It was then that they heard a snarling voice exclaim, 'You festering fools! You blinded, bumbling bunglers! I told you to bring them all!'

'But, sir!' replied one of the guards, 'we did!'

'I told you, I made it plain, repeated it thrice, that you were to bring Ursus Major, the Great Bear!'

'But we thought we had!' answered the guard, gesturing towards Mr Goodman. 'It was difficult to see in the smoke and the dark and this was a big shape and so, naturally, we assumed . . .'

'I don't know who this corpulent idiot is,' exclaimed Malevil, glaring at Mr Goodman, 'but he is *not* the Great Bear! You have let him escape. We need him here to interpret *The Book of Merlin*. You shall pay for this folly. Bring him here at once, do you understand? At once!'

Malevil, having vented his anger, turned back to the small band of friends.

'As for the others,' he smiled, 'you shall shortly have the pleasure of simmering in Merlin's Cauldron while we await the arrival of your friend, Ursus Major!'

He turned to the guards at his side.

'Summon everyone immediately to the Council Chamber, and bring the prisoners with you. It is time for a council of war!'

Even as Malevil was speaking, the Great Bear was travelling at full speed along an underground passage, accompanied by Taliesin, on his way to the inside of the mountain.

When the smoke had begun to fill the room he had realised at once what was happening. The smoke was being injected down the chimney, while the windows and doors had been barricaded from outside by Malevil's men. Swiftly he had stepped into the fireplace and through the smoke which now hid him from the intruders. He waited in a recess there until the others had been taken. As soon as he heard the van drive off, he called softly to Taliesin and, lifting a flagstone in the floor of the hearth, climbed down a flight of steps that led to an underground passage. At the end of this passage was an oak door, covered with dust and cobwebs. Taking a bunch of keys from his waist, he tried several, until he found the one that fitted. Once on the other side, he locked the door so that no one could follow after him.

The tunnel descended in a zigzag. Soon he came to

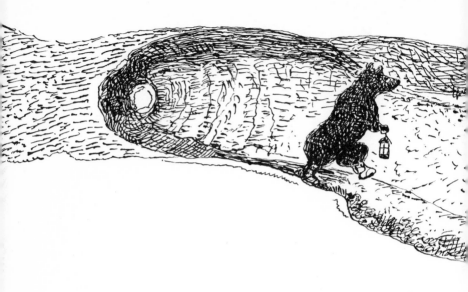

another door. There were seven of these doors. The tunnel and the doors had been built for Merlin so that he might have a private entrance to the mountain, but neither the tunnel nor the doors had been used for centuries. Taliesin and the Great Bear passed through them, one after the other, until they came to the seventh, the wood of which was so damp that the ancient oak had rotted away.

The Great Bear extinguished the lantern he had been carrying and stood in the darkness, waiting and listening. From now on he would have to rely on his memory of the many paths inside the mountain, upon his sense of smell, and upon Taliesin. He moved cautiously, his senses as alert as those of a blind man, knowing that the slightest sound would echo and give away his presence. It was up to him now to rescue the others but, first, he had to find out what was happening.

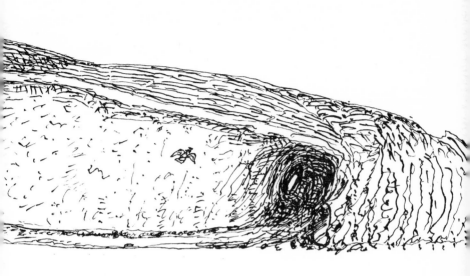

After a time he began to hear the distant roar of a waterfall and knew that he must be nearing the centre of the mountain. Soon he could hear voices and the throb of electric generators. The sound seemed to be coming from the Great Assembly Chamber which Merlin had had cut out of the rock for the secret meetings of the Knights of the Round Table.

The Great Bear paused. Somewhere, close at hand, he remembered, there was an entrance to a smaller chamber high up in the roof of the Great Chamber, from which Merlin had been able to observe the secret meetings of the Round Table. Its presence had been known only to Merlin and the Great Bear.

Carefully he felt along the rock surface until he found what he was looking for – a smooth slab of rock between two craggy pillars. Reaching up to the tops of the two pillars he pressed downwards. Nothing happened.

At that moment, round a bend in the tunnel, lights flashed. Two guards were approaching. Swiftly Taliesin flew towards them in order to create a distraction while the Great Bear made another attempt to find the mechanism that operated the opening in the rock surface.

'There's a barn owl got in here, Sid! Do you see?' shouted one of the men.

'How'd he get in, then?'

'How'd yer think?' answered the first guard. 'Same way as you and me, mate. And I'm telling you this – he won't get out any more than we shall! This ruddy mountain's getting on my nerves!'

Sweat was running down the hairs on the Great Bear's face as the guards moved nearer. Once again he pressed downwards on the two pillars, his muscles straining. He knew that no magic could open the door, merely the exact amount of pressure on the right spot. It was a knack and he was out of practice.

'Come on, Sid!' called the first guard. 'Else we'll be late for the Assembly.'

'Hey, look out!' shouted the other guard as Taliesin began to dive-bomb the two men. Both ducked in terror. At that moment the Great Bear felt the rock in front of him slowly rise, revealing a flight of steps. As he entered, the slab automatically closed behind him.

Round and round he climbed. He had forgotten how high the spiral staircase went, so high was the hall of the Assembly Chamber. The noise of voices was louder now, echoing and reverberating as he climbed, until he seemed to be at the centre of the sound. Suddenly it cleared and he found himself in a small chamber with a narrow slit in the rock from which he could look down,

unseen, on the Great Hall below.

What he saw startled him. Until now he had not fully realised the extent of Malevil's resources.

The Assembly Chamber that, centuries ago, had been lit by rush lamps, was now floodlit by arc lamps. Through the massive doors into the hall filed the men of Malevil. In their stark uniforms and shiny peaked caps with the insignia of a single eye, the mark of Malevil, they hurried into the chamber like black beetles. At one end, on a dais carved out of the rock, stood Malevil. At his side, escorted by guards, and with their arms bound behind their backs, stood Odd, Mr Goodman, Hallelujah and Farmer Thomas.

When all the men, in their hundreds, were standing, rank upon rank, waiting silently, Ratzwill raised his arm and cried out –

See no evil but Malevil!

And in that great Assembly Chamber where, so long ago, the Knights of the Round Table had pledged their oaths, the men of Malevil now pledged themselves to their leader:

See no evil but Malevil!
Hear no evil but Malevil!
Speak no evil but Malevil!

The Great Bear leaned forward in order to see more clearly. As he did so, his foot knocked against a pile of loose stones which rattled forward along the narrow aperture through which he was looking, and fell, curving through the air, upon the startled, up-turned faces below.

The sudden shower of stones caused the main body of men in the Chamber below to scatter in panic. Malevil peered up into the high vaulted roof and frowned.

The stones could just be a landslide, he thought, caused perhaps by the reverberations of the many hundreds of voices ringing out, or it could be . . .

'Ratzwill!' His voice snapped like the hard thud of a bullet from a rifle.

'Sir?' answered Ratzwill, marching forward and standing to attention.

'Get your men out of here at once, let them search all the adjoining tunnels and passages. There may be hidden chambers in the rock, especially above this hall. And take the prisoners at once to Merlin's Cauldron. I have a feeling that this landslide may have been caused by our mutual enemy, the Great Bear. He must be found at all costs, Ratzwill. Do you understand? Now! At once!'

Although Malevil whispered these last words, the Great Bear heard them as clearly as a peal of bells. Swiftly he turned and left the secret chamber and hurried down the spiral staircase. At the bottom he groped once again for the mechanism that would open the slab of rock that formed the entrance to the tunnel outside. He could hear many sounds echoing, as though huge armies were on the march. His head was splitting with the noise. His paws fumbled clumsily in the dark. He realised he was frightened. His sight was not what it had been; his memory was faulty; and his feet were troubling him from old wounds that had never properly healed.

As the slab of rock slid up, he felt the stirring of air on his face and heard a flutter of wings. It was Taliesin. At the same moment lights flashed and voices rang out: 'There he is!'

At once Taliesin rose up and dived in to attack as the

Great Bear stumbled forward, away from the guards, and in the direction of Merlin's Chapel. At all costs he had to avoid being caught, since now only he was left to rescue the others from the dreaded Merlin's Cauldron. Already an idea was forming in his brain, but there was little time in which to carry it out. In spite of Taliesin's assistance, the guards were already gaining ground on him. He ran, paws outstretched, breathing heavily.

He reached the entrance to the tunnel that led up to the hermitage, and hurried in, locking each door behind him, in the hope that this would give him the extra time which he needed desperately if he was to put his plan into operation.

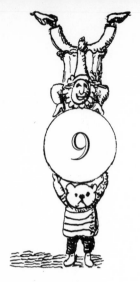

Elsewhere's caravan drew up outside Merlin's Chapel. He had taken the short cut through the Forest from Tippity House. He tethered the horse to the wooden fence and walked up the garden path, looking at the neat rows of vegetables in the Great Bear's garden. The sun was only just up and the bees were not yet at work. The door of the Chapel stood open but there was no sign of anyone about.

Elsewhere knocked.

'Are you up, Odd?' he called.

He knocked again and went in.

The inside looked as though it had been ransacked by thieves; tables and chairs were overthrown, books ripped apart, while a fine black soot lay over everything. It looked, thought Elsewhere, as though there had been a fire.

Suddenly he heard a series of explosions. Bang! Bang-bang-bang! Bang! BANG! He ran outside and there, twisting in and out of the trees of the Forest travelled a very old car, snorting and hissing, with the words 'The Love Bug' gaily painted across it. Seated at the wheel was a tiny little man wearing a crash helmet and goggles. The car shuddered to a standstill, steam rising from the bonnet. The driver honked his hooter cheerfully and climbed out, removing his helmet and goggles. 'Arbuthnot!' cried Elsewhere with delight, going to greet him. Arbuthnot was Mr Goodman's assistant.

'Why, it's Elsewhere!' answered Arbuthnot, warmly shaking his hand. 'I didn't know you were back from your travels. How are you? Is Odd with you?'

Elsewhere explained that he had come to collect Odd for a picnic with the Welsh clowns but that there seemed to be no sign of anyone about.

'Perhaps he and Hallelujah went back with Farmer Thomas to the farm,' said Elsewhere. 'What are you doing here?'

'I've called to see what has happened to Mr Goodman,' explained Arbuthnot. 'He drove off to market yesterday and we haven't seen him since.'

The two strolled round to the back of the hermitage.

'There's the Granary van!' exclaimed Arbuthnot. 'Then Mr Goodman must have come on here from the market.'

'And that's Farmer Thomas's land-rover!' added Elsewhere. 'So they must be around somewhere. It's very strange.'

They went into the house together and stood looking at the wreckage.

'It's as deserted as a nest when the bird is flown,' observed Arbuthnot.

The logs on the hearth were charred to smouldering ashes and a thin thread of smoke rose up the chimney.

'Look out!' cried Elsewhere sharply, ducking, as a large black bat flew out of the fireplace towards them. Instead of wheeling out through the open door the bat perched on top of the dresser and hooted.

'That's funny!' said Arbuthnot. 'I've never seen a bat that size before. Nor one that hooted. I wonder . . .'

He stopped. From the back of the fireplace emerged a tall figure, black and grimy as a miner coming up from the pit.

Whooo-oo! Whooo-oo! went the bat.

At that moment Arbuthnot and Elsewhere realised it was Taliesin and—

66

'Great Bear!' cried Elsewhere, going to greet him. 'Where have you been? And where are the others?'

'There's no time to be lost!' grunted the Great Bear. 'Follow me!'

Taking the large key from the front door he charged up the garden path. Holding the key above each of the hives in turn, he talked to the bees. He told them how the others had been captured by Malevil and were imprisoned inside the mountain. 'I want you to bring help,' he finished, 'as soon as possible!'

He paused. Inside the hives the humming of the bees grew louder and angrier as though the hives were about to boil over. From the entrance to each, bees began to trickle forth. Like twelve plumes of smoke the bees rose up from the twelve hives, forming twelve small clouds which merged into one cloud of thousands of bees.

'They're hovering like starlings in autumn,' observed Arbuthnot. The next moment the bees had vanished.

'They'll be back,' answered the Great Bear chuckling, 'and with reinforcements! Now, I must hide. Any moment Malevil's men will break through the last door under the chapel and they must not find me. The question is – *where* can I hide?'

'In my caravan!' answered Elsewhere promptly. 'Malevil doesn't know of my existence nor of my connection with you. So get in quickly. Both of you!' he added, turning to Arbuthnot.

While the two climbed on board, Elsewhere quickly removed his cap, darkened his face with some burned corks, fixed a curtain ring to one ear, then tied a colourful scarf around his forehead. In no time at all he was transformed into a gipsy. He picked up the reins and the caravan moved forward.

From inside the hermitage came loud shouts and the next moment several guards ran out.

'Stop!' shouted one to Elsewhere who reined in and brought the caravan to a standstill.

'Heather! White heather for sale!' cried Elsewhere in a cracked voice. 'Bring you good luck! Tell your fortune for you!'

'Ruddy gipsies!' muttered the guard.

A second guard shouted up at Elsewhere. 'Have you seen a bear lately?'

'Have I seen a bare what?' asked Elsewhere.

'No! Have you seen a *bear*, a real bear? Large furry creature!'

Elsewhere shook his head, the big curtain ring swinging.

'No bears round these parts,' he answered. 'Not for a hundred years. Last one seen round here escaped from a circus. Was stoned to death. No bears today!'

The second guard whispered to the first, 'Ask him what he's got in the back. Can't trust these gipsies.'

'What you got in the back there?' asked the first guard.

'Only the missis and her baby,' answered Elsewhere. 'She's sick. Taking her into town to get some medicine.'

'You'd better search the caravan just in case,' said the second guard to the first.

'You won't find any bears in here!' grinned Elsewhere.

The guard climbed up onto the caravan and Elsewhere opened the door so that he could see inside. At the far end, on the bunk bed, under a small window the curtains of which were drawn, the guard could just make out two shapes, one large, one small, under the blankets. The larger shape was groaning while the smaller cried like a baby.

'I shouldn't go too close if I were you,' said Elsewhere. 'I think it's scarlet fever. Mind you, I don't know for certain.'

'Fever!' repeated the first guard. 'That's all we want now, an epidemic of fever!'

Quickly he jumped down. 'Thanks, gippo!' he called out to Elsewhere.

Elsewhere took up the reins and the caravan moved slowly off through the trees. Looking back, he could see the guards fanning out into the Forest, in search of the Great Bear. He called over his shoulder to the interior of the caravan, 'All clear! You can come out!'

From under the blankets emerged the Great Bear and Arbuthnot. Elsewhere grinned at them.

'Those groans were very realistic!' he said.

'I should think they were!' chuckled the Great Bear. 'I had to stuff the pillow in my mouth to stop myself laughing! I've never heard such a noise as Arbuthnot was making!'

'And now what?' asked Arbuthnot, perching beside Elsewhere.

'I think that instead of a picnic,' answered Elsewhere, 'we'll turn the Gathering of Welsh Clowns into a rescue party. I've got a plan. Now, as soon as we get to Tippity House, I want you, Arbuthnot, to go down to the village shop and get six tins of beeswax—'

'Six tins of beeswax,' repeated Arbuthnot, writing it down in a little notebook.

'As many marbles as you can find . . .'

'As many marbles . . .' repeated Arbuthnot.

'Some reels of black thread . . .'

'Reels of black thread,' repeated Arbuthnot.

'And a skeleton,' added Elsewhere.

'A skeleton?' echoed Arbuthnot. 'I shan't be able to buy a skeleton at the village shop!'

'Well look in the cupboards when we get back to Tippity House! There's always skeletons in cupboards.'

'One skeleton,' wrote Arbuthnot in his notebook.

'Fools! Imbeciles! And Innate Idiots!' muttered Malevil.

He was pacing up and down and around. Each time he thought he had stolen a march on the enemy he had succeeded only in slipping back. He had successfully moved his troops into the mountain under cover of darkness, only to give away his presence in the neighbourhood by speaking to Odd. He had succeeded in securing *The Book of Merlin* but had failed to capture the Great Bear without whose aid he could not hope to decipher the code. Then, lastly, the Great Bear had been seen inside the mountain and yet, somehow, in spite of all Malevil's forces, he had escaped.

Malevil sat slumped in his chair. His eyeball was throbbing painfully. He felt old and drained and tired. He wondered whether the long pursuit of the Treasure over so many centuries had not been in vain. Like the Lost Treasure of El Dorado it might never be discovered. Perhaps, after all, thought Malevil, he should give up now, and let others carry on the search if they wanted. But who was there? Ratzwill? The thought of Ratzwill benefiting from his long labours pulled him up with a jerk. He was not going to give up so easily!

The Book of Merlin lay before him: so much meaning-less jumbo without the necessary key. Meanwhile the Great Bear was at large. His first task was to find and capture him and then force him to surrender the key to the code. But how to go about it? He knew that how-ever strong his forces, they were at a disadvantage once the Great Bear was inside the mountain. He had no doubt that the Great Bear could successfully elude them for days, weeks even. Malevil had too much respect for the Great Bear's canniness to expect that he would be easily captured unless . . . and here Malevil paused. A thin smile thawed his grim expression. The one thing that could be relied upon to get the Great Bear into his net was, in fact, the presence of Odd and the other members of the small band within the moun-tain. The Great Bear would be sure to make an attempt to rescue them.

Malevil lifted the internal telephone and said, 'Send me the Captain of the Guard.'

As he sat there waiting, the smile spread across his face until he was almost grinning.

'Sir!' The Captain of the Guard stood to attention and saluted.

'Stand at ease, Captain!'

'Sir!'

'How are the prisoners faring?'

'We've no trouble from the small bear, sir, but Mr Jones is a bit of a handful. He's very religious. Always shouting out – *Hallelujah*! *Praise the Lord*! and *Amen*! It's getting the men down. We'll have to gag him if he goes on like that.'

'How many men have you got on guard at the moment?'

'Four, sir.'

'I want you to treble that number, Captain. But keep the eight new guards out of sight. Here is the plan I want you to put into operation at once – It's Operation U.M.2.'

'Operation U.M.2, sir?'

'Yes, Captain. Operation Ursus Major – It must not fail or you will all be shot!'

Abruptly the door of the headquarters burst open and Ratzwill entered.

'What is it, Ratzwill?' snapped Malevil.

'Sir, sir, sir!' stammered Ratzwill nervously, tugging at the hairs inside his right nostril.

'For my sake,' exclaimed Malevil, 'stop twirling! And tell me calmly what is the matter.'

'It's the men, sir.'

'What about them?'

'We seem to have lost about half our force, sir!'

'*Lost*!' cried Malevil. 'You don't just *lose* men, Ratzwill, or if you do, you will lose *your* head! Explain yourself!'

'The truth is,' continued Ratzwill, 'the mountain has been invaded.'

'*Invaded*!' screamed Malevil. 'Why did you not tell me this immediately. Invaded? By whom?'

'Some of the men are saying it is bats, sir. There have been reports of a giant bat swooping and attacking the men. He goes for their eyes, sir.'

Instinctively Malevil put a hand in front of his one eye.

'Go on, Ratzwill!' he said, listening now attentively.

'Others say that they have seen Merlin himself, sir, and . . .' Here Ratzwill paused, twirling at the hairs in his left ear.

'Well, go on!' shouted Malevil.

'I don't know how to say this, sir, but many of the men have been stung. The men all say it is Merlin's magic and that it comes of the mountain being haunted.'

Malevil stared at Ratzwill, his one eyeball bulging, and the vertical frown on his forehead deepening into a hard black line. He rose quietly.

'You'd better show me what you mean, Ratzwill,' he said. Turning to the Captain he added, 'You come with us as well.'

Ratzwill led the way down various tunnels. Suddenly Malevil stopped. Ahead of them, in a clearing, were clouds of what appeared to be black smoke. The air vibrated with a humming sound. Terrified screams echoed along the passageways as Malevil's men fled from the black smoke.

'What is that noise? What are those cries? What is that smoke?' whispered Malevil in awe.

'Those are the cries of our men, sir, being stung by the bees. That is not smoke but swarms of bees. The mountain is swarming with bees. There must be millions of them. Goodness knows where they have come from. And bees such as I have never seen before. The men are so terrified that they just run, anywhere, and fall headlong over precipices or into underground rivers. It's as though the inside of the mountain were flooded with bees.'

'Quick!' said Malevil, turning swiftly to the Captain of the Guard. 'I know whose handiwork this is. This is indeed Merlin's Magic. It is the Great Bear's doing and, if we do not act immediately, it will be our *un*doing. Our only chance now is to catch him while he is trying to free the others from Merlin's Cauldron. That will be his next task. Hurry! We have no time to lose!'

'Our only way out,' said Mr Goodman to Odd, staring upwards, 'is to climb the chain.'

'We don't really stand a chance, do we?' said Farmer Thomas quietly to Hallelujah.

The four friends were suspended in a huge cauldron above a deep chasm. The cauldron was operated by means of a chain on a pulley that was situated high in the roof of the cavern where the guards kept watch.

In the bottom of the chasm burned a fire of dampened peats that sent up clouds of thick smoke which brought tears to the eyes of those in the cauldron. The cauldron had been invented by Merlin as a combined prison and torture chamber for the enemies of King Arthur.

'Of course,' observed Mr Goodman to Farmer Thomas, 'if you were to stand on my shoulders you might be able to reach the chain. The smoke will help to conceal you from the guards above.'

He cupped his hands in front of him and Farmer Thomas climbed up onto his shoulders. Odd and Hallelujah helped to steady Mr Goodman as the cauldron rocked with the movement. They could hear

Farmer Thomas struggling but Odd, staring up through the smoke, could see nothing. Being so small he was much farther down in the pit of the cauldron.

'It's no good!' gasped Farmer Thomas, slithering back down. 'I can't get a grip on the chain. My hands keep slipping and the links of the chain are too small for me to get my fingers in.'

The friends stood, dispirited and damp with weeping, inside the great cauldron. Their eyes were red and inflamed from the smoke and they were tired from lack of sleep.

'Might I have a try?' asked Odd quietly.

The others looked at him.

'But you're not tall enough to reach the chain, boy bach,' replied Hallelujah kindly.

'No, but if Farmer Thomas were to stand on Mr Goodman's shoulders and you were to stand on Farmer Thomas's shoulders, like they do in the circus, I think then I should be able to reach.'

'But if I couldn't get a grip on the chain,' argued Farmer Thomas, 'how will you manage? After all you've always said your paws are not very good for gripping.'

'I know, but I've been learning to use my claws,' answered Odd. 'And where you can't get your fingers into the links, I think my claws might fit. That way I could climb to the top and perhaps wind you all up to the platform there.'

'We'll try it, lad!' answered Farmer Thomas energetically, although he did not have much hope of Odd's success.

He climbed up onto Mr Goodman's shoulders, and Hallelujah, who was much more agile since the Great

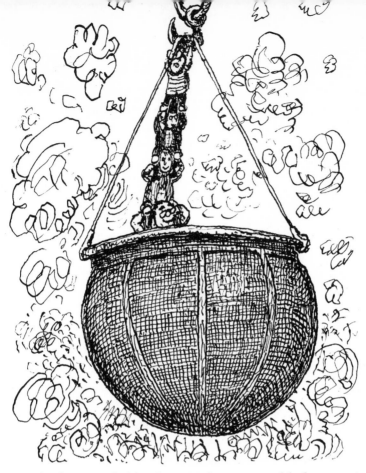

Bear had treated his rheumatism, scrambled up onto his shoulders.

Carefully, so as not to overbalance them, Odd pulled himself up the human pillar. Standing on Hallelujah's shoulders he found himself well above the mouth of the cauldron. Above him the chain stretched away into the ascending smoke and darkness. Slowly he began to climb, hooking his claws into the links of the chain.

Soon he had left behind his friends. He could see neither up nor down and he had no idea of how much farther he had to climb.

He paused for a moment. The pain in his arms, as well as the soreness in his eyes from the smoke, was so fierce that he felt he could not go on. The farther he climbed the farther there would be to fall if his arms gave out. Suddenly, up there in the dark, out in space, he was frightened. He had no more strength left. He had tried but the odds had been against him.

It was then, just when he was about to give up, that he seemed to see, so clearly, the face of the Great Bear, and with this vision of his friend there came a strange calm. Although he was exhausted, he felt new strength inside himself. It's telepathy, thought Odd. The Great Bear seemed to be saying something to him but he could not quite catch the words. He knew, however, that he must go on, that he would go on. He had only to climb and to concentrate on one move at a time. He must not think how far he had come nor how far he might have to go. He must just keep climbing.

Arm over arm, he climbed, until, at last, he could hear voices. He had reached the underside of the platform where the pulley was and where the guards kept watch. From where he hung, Odd could hear without being seen.

'I wish I hadn't signed on with this lot,' said one of the guards. 'It was the uniform took my fancy.'

'I joined for the money,' said a second. 'And besides, I thought I'd see some action.'

'Hah!' answered the first guard. 'Some ruddy action we've seen cooped up inside this mountain for weeks on end.'

'I reckon this mountain is haunted,' said a third guard. 'You should hear some of the stories I've heard about it in the Drovers' Arms. Folks round here call it the Black Mountain. They won't go near it. They say too many people have come to a nasty end on it. They say it is haunted by Merlin.'

Odd frowned. He could hear a noise like that of wind blowing down many chimneys. Then he heard a pipe fluting and strings vibrating, an eerie music filling the great cavern with echoes.

'Blimey!' cried one of the guards. 'The mountain *is* haunted!'

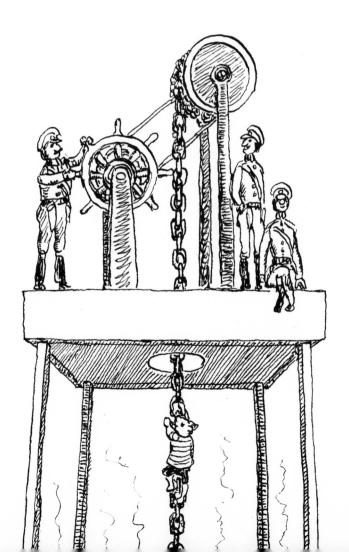

'Ghosts!' cried another.

'I'm off!' cried a third.

'Wait for me!' shouted the last.

Pulling himself up, Odd peered over the top of the platform and gasped. Moving slowly along the tunnel was a huge white horse with an enormous head that towered in the air. The horse appeared to have no legs but slowly rose and fell as though it were floating.

The guards ran, skidding and tumbling into each other. As soon as they were out of sight the strange music ceased and the horse began to wobble like a blancmange. There was a sound of giggling. From underneath, appeared several small figures, some carrying musical instruments. It was then that Odd saw that the horse was made from sheets sewn together, with two large buttons for the eyes, and a pair of leather gardening gloves for the ears. The head was stuffed with straw and supported on the end of a pitchfork.

The small figures ran about, laughing and shouting, *Cymru yn byth* and *Wales for ever*! At the same moment a voice cried out, 'All right! All right! There's no need to get carried away. Talk about over-acting!'

At once the clowns stood still.

'Elsewhere!' cried Odd.

'Odd!' cried Elsewhere running to drag his friend up onto the platform. At the same moment Hywel-ap-Hywel stepped forward, grinning at Odd. 'Hullo, boy bach! You all right then?'

Odd nodded.

Elsewhere called to Llewellyn to wind up the cauldron as quickly as he could. 'The rest of you,' he said to Hywel-ap-Hywel, 'clear this stuff out of the way, keep out of sight, and alert the others to stand by.'

'The others?' said Odd.

'Yes!' laughed Elsewhere. 'We've brought an entire Gathering to your rescue!'

Swiftly Llewellyn turned the handle of the pulley and slowly the cauldron rose up through the smoke.

'I never thought you'd make it, Odd!' said Mr Goodman as he climbed out, followed by Farmer Thomas and Hallelujah.

'Well done, lad!' said Farmer Thomas.

'Well done, boy bach!' added Hallelujah.

Suddenly an icy voice rang out. 'Not quite well enough done, my friend!'

For a moment everyone froze like a scene in a wax-work tableau. At the foot of the staircase leading to the platform stood Malevil. In his hand he held something black and glittering. With him was Ratzwill, followed by the Captain of the guard.

'Don't move or I shoot,' said Malevil. 'And I shoot to kill!'

Then, from the darkness of the main tunnel behind Malevil, a deeper voice chuckled, 'Dear me! Such melodrama!'

Malevil at once swung round to where the Great Bear stood, but, before he could raise his gun, Taliesin had swooped and knocked it from his hand. Elsewhere and some of the Welsh clowns struggled with Ratzwill and the Captain of the guard. Malevil let out a cry as Taliesin swooped on him again, aiming for his eye. For a moment Malevil hesitated then he turned and disappeared down a side passage.

'After him at once!' shouted the Great Bear to Elsewhere. 'Don't leave him inside the Mountain!'

Elsewhere turned to Hywel-ap-Hywel who took his flute and blew a long single note.

'But where is everybody?' asked Odd, puzzled.

'No time for questions now!' answered Elsewhere. 'Follow me!'

Malevil ran. He was none too sure where he was running to although he knew that he was running away. He had been unnerved by the sight and sound of the bees, as well as by Taliesin swooping upon him; above all, by the fact that, once again, just as he had been on the point of winning, he had been foiled.

As he ran he was conscious that he was not alone. He could hear whisperings, scurrying noises, an occasional rattle of stones. Then he began to hear voices, or was he imagining them? beckoning him on, now in this direction, now in that. '*Malevil, Malevil, give us a call!*' they repeated, '*A pee-weep whistle or nothing at all!*'

He was running along a low tunnel when 'things' began to happen. The floor beneath him suddenly seemed to give way, to glide forward, as hundreds and hundreds of small round stones rolled under his feet. He fell and went sprawling. Reaching out his arms to try and break his fall, his hands clutched at what felt, in the darkness, like glass eyes.

He did not know that all along the tunnel, stationed at intervals, were clowns, each with a bag of marbles, which they rolled onto the ground as Malevil came slithering and stumbling forward.

At last, however, he was clear of that tunnel and running, with thumping heart and bruised knees, up a steepening slope. He could no longer hear the whispering, mocking voices. For a moment he paused. It appeared that he had left them behind. He slowed down in order to regain his breath. By now he had reached the top of the slope, but he had no torch and it was so dark that he could not see his hands as they reached forward to feel the ground ahead of him. It appeared now to slope downwards. Slowly he moved forward, in a shuffling movement, his hands tracing the walls of the tunnel on either side. Once again his feet gave way beneath him. He slipped, fell on his bottom and began to slide down the slope, twisting and turning as though he were on a helter-skelter. He could have sworn that

someone had deliberately polished the stone floor. As he skidded and swerved, down and around, faster and faster, he could hear the voices again all about him in the darkness.

'It's trolls!' muttered Malevil. 'Mountain trolls! And goblins!' He had never believed in such things but now he was convinced that mischievous sprites were at work. Either that, or this was, indeed, the magic of Merlin.

At the end of the slippery slope he came to a cave in a far corner of which he could see a light. There was an opening in the rock through which he passed. At the same moment the light went out. Once again he was in the dark.

Ah! He screamed with fright, as a large skeleton appeared in front of him, lit by a flickering torch. He did not know that the skeleton was suspended by strong black thread from a long pole, held by one of the clowns. Another clown flickered a torch on and off. The skeleton vanished. The next moment it re-appeared behind Malevil, its long arms reaching out to envelop him. He ran, terrified, faster and faster. Faster and faster ran the skeleton while all around him he could hear the voices cat-calling, hooting, making owl-calls and bat-squeaks, accompanied by a blowing of whistles, a rattling of gourds, a ringing of bells, such a pandemonium of sound that the mountain echoed and re-echoed with it.

Malevil was deafened and bewildered by the noise. He had lost all sense of direction and just ran aimlessly.

He had been running for more than an hour when at long last the sounds stopped. There was nothing but the huge silence of the mountain and the roar of water from a waterfall somewhere close at hand.

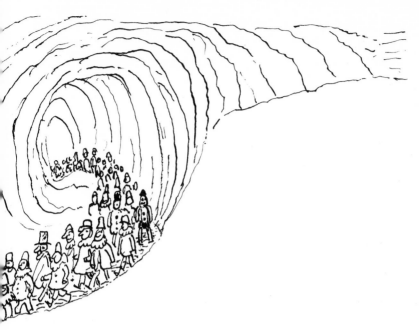

He came out into a large arena, and at the far end was a ravine into which thundered seven waterfalls. A faint light illumined the scene. Across the ravine were seven bridges one of which was broken. Each bridge appeared to lead straight through one of the waterfalls. Malevil hesitated, wondering which bridge to take, when a noise made him swing round. He saw that he was surrounded by hundreds and hundreds of silent small figures dressed in white, their deep set eyes glittering in the soft light. They fanned out in a circle around him. He did not know who they were nor where they had come from. Then he saw, at a distance, Ursus Minor and his friends, and, farther back, in the shadows, the towering figure of the Great Bear.

Malevil's last stand was a brave one. He took on the entire Gathering of Clowns with a ferocity and a passion of despair that took them by surprise. But in the end he knew that he was beaten. The sweat poured down his face, causing his eye to smart. He ached in every limb, while his chest rose and fell rapidly as though his heart were out of control.

The clowns stood ranged before him. They, too, were bruised, bloodied, and badly shaken.

Everyone stood waiting. Odd looked around at them in the flickering, dim light of the huge chamber. He looked at the Great Bear and saw that he, too, appeared to be listening for something. It was almost as if they were all awaiting a signal. It was then, in the silence, that he heard a sound. Soon the others heard it also. It seemed to be coming from above them, at the summit of the mountain. As they listened it grew stronger and nearer. It was the sound of many voices singing, of people on the march. In the darkness of the plateau, beyond and behind the clowns, the singing swelled. Now tongues of fire appeared, the lights of flaming torches, lighting up the darkness, creating vast shadows. A river of many flames began to pour out of a tunnel and to move rhythmically across the open space. The voices swelled, like those of boys singing in a choir.

Malevil was forgotten as the clowns turned to face the approaching army. But it was Odd who first recognised them. Hundreds upon hundreds of small bears were filing out of the tunnel and massing themselves in ranks. They came to a halt, their brown eyes glowing in the light from their torches.

Odd stepped forward.

'I am Ursus Minor,' he said. 'Who are you?'

'We,' answered one of the small bears, 'are the Treasure of Wales. We got tired of waiting. So we deci-

ded to come and look for you. The mists on top of the
mountain have cleared and we thought you might have
forgotten to come and look for us!'

There was a sudden commotion as Malevil pushed his
way through the clowns, elbowing Odd to one side.

'What's this you are saying?' he shouted. 'What's
this nonsense about you being the Treasure?'

'That is right,' answered the small bear.

'You mean to say,' cried Malevil, 'that the Treasure
is nothing but a load of small bears? Or is this some jest
of Merlin's?'

'It is no jest,' said a deep voice quietly. The Great
Bear emerged from the shadows. 'Here, indeed, is the
Lost Treasure of Wales. Not gold, nor silver nor precious
stones, but a new race of Welsh bears. And Odd is their
leader!'

'You fool!' shouted Malevil. 'Why did you not tell me
this before? Why did you let me believe the treasure
was what I thought it to be?'

'I never said what the Treasure was, answered the Great Bear, 'because I had truly forgotten. Merlin had taken good care that I should not remember until the time was ripe! Even had I known, however, I doubt that you would have believed me.'

'Nothing but a hug of bears!' muttered Malevil.

'Nothing but!' repeated the Great Bear. 'And yet, as you will discover one day, of more value than your precious gold and silver!'

Odd looked up at the Great Bear, smiling.

'And to think that, only the other day, Collander Moll called *me* a treasure and I never guessed even then!'

He stopped speaking. The bears were opening their ranks. They moved apart to allow Malevil to pass through their midst. No one attempted to stop him. In silence, with only the thunder of the seven waterfalls echoing in that great chamber, the Gathering of Clowns and the Hug of Bears watched Malevil pass from them.

'He cannot hurt anyone now!' said the Great Bear gently. 'It is right that we should let him go.'

93

When they came out at the top of the mountain there was no sign anywhere of Malevil. The sun had risen and the mists had lifted from the summit. There, reflected in the waters of the lake, against a brilliant sky, rose the Castle of Merlin, its towers reaching upwards like the outstretched fingers of a hand.

Buzzards circled in the sky. Looking down the mountain Odd could see people arriving. Trestle tables had been set up in the main courtyard of the castle and Collander Moll was covering them with cloths, assisted by Mrs Thomas and the children. Dr Morgan and his wife arrived carrying hampers of food.

The bears came trooping out, and now Odd could see them more clearly. They looked exactly like him and yet each was different in shade, colour, and shape, just as people are alike but different. Some were laughing and chattering excitedly like small boys at the end of term looking forward to the holidays, some moved forward shyly and uncertainly, others raced forward eager to be up and doing, some looked back wistfully at the mountain which they would soon be leaving for ever.

They all gathered around Odd to hear from him the whole story of how he had first come to learn about the Great Bear and then made up his mind to find him, of

their encounters with Malevil, and how in the end it had been his friend Elsewhere who had come to their rescue.

As he spoke, Odd looked across at Elsewhere, who was on the other side of the courtyard rehearsing something for the party with the other clowns.

Someone was playing a harp. Odd saw that it was Collander Moll's auntie, Miss Myfanwy. More people were still arriving for the picnic and now he recognised a familiar figure crossing the courtyard towards him deep in conversation with the Great Bear. It was the old King of the Clowns whom Elsewhere had succeeded.

'You've come into your own, then, at last!' said the old King to him. 'Both you and Elsewhere.'

The music broke into a dance tune and at once all the bears, brown and grey, and white and black and golden, were dancing arm in arm with the clowns, winding in and out, and on and on. Odd took Elsewhere's hand and they all formed a great circle, while Taliesin rose up in their midst towards the sun as it rose higher and higher above Merlin's Castle on Bear Mountain.